Phillip and Mimi

Mark Albini

Published in the United States of America

ISBN 978-1-962569-50-7 (SC)
ISBN 978-1-962730-96-9 (HC)

Mark Albini Publishing
155 weeping Willow Dr.,
Myrtle Beach South Carolina 29579
rhyminganimaladventures@yahoo.com.

Order Information and Rights Permission:

Quantity sales. Special discounts might be available on quantity purchases by corporations, associations, and others. For details, contact the publisher at the address above.

For Book Rights Adaptation and other Rights Permission.
Call us at toll-free 1-888-945-8513 or send us an email at
admin@stellarliterary.com

A Special Thank You to my wife, Sharyn Albini, who had to listen to all the writes and rewrites over the years.

Dedicated to my parents, Louis Alfred Albini, Katherine Jeannine Albini and DJT.

Inspired by my love for animals, my love for America, my father Louis Albini, and Clement C. Moore.

Honoring my Christian Faith, my good friends and a few people from the past who were special to me. I've used their names as the names of my characters in the Rescue Ranch Series. I had so many friends with the name Bob I had to use the name Bobo to cover them all. They became the voice of wisdom on the farm and it was a fun way to keep my friends around me. This way we could all live forever in the stories. I won't get them all in but I'm going to try.

The Creation of Rescue Ranch

It all began the day Grandpa Eddie purchased an old farmhouse that sat on a large parcel of land. The farmhouse was a few hundred miles from an old country zoo he used to visit as a boy. The zoo was closing after its caretaker had passed away but a family member stayed on to run the zoo until she could find a home for the animals. The Giraffes were chosen to be the first to go. Grandpa Eddie agreed to take the Giraffe family and drove up to the old farmhouse just in time to see the Giraffes arrive. They were dropped off in a field that backed up to an old red barn across the street from the house. Jimmy was excited to have a new home but surprised to find out he had to get up early. Tomorrow was a school day. On his way there he passed a shed with a beautiful white horse named Howie. Howie became Jimmy's best friend and on most days Jimmy would stop by in the morning and they would walk to school together. Some of the buildings they passed along the way had been rundown for years and it was obvious there was a lot to do on this old farm. Grandpa Eddie woke up early everyday of his life and went right to work. He needed to make room for some of the animals he was hoping to rescue. He planted some crops, cleaned out the barn and went looking for a hog to put in the sty. It didn't take long before it started to feel like home. He decided to call it The Rescue Ranch.

Introduction

The Rescue Ranch is a peaceful place where animals live in wide open space.

They're fed everyday and have plenty to eat. Life on this farm is really quite sweet.

It's a place for animals to come and stay and meet new friends and have fun each day.

The animals are friendly and very sincere and most have retired from a long career.

Except for those who were born on the farm and a few in the woods that have caused alarm

If they live in the woods or somewhere on the farm they all contribute to its countryside charm.

So welcome to the Rescue Ranch where animals receive an olive branch.

BOOK #1   Jimmy the Giraffe
BOOK #2   Ricky the Rabbit
and Bobo the Mouse
BOOK #3   Terry the Turtle
and Freddie the Fish
BOOK #4   Sammy the Snake
BOOK #5   Philip and Mimi
BOOK #6   Henry the Hog --- COMING SOON!

RESCUE
RANCH

Phillip the Frog got a really big break
when he got away clean from Sammy the Snake
'Twas Terry the Turtle who warned me away
when Sammy went searching for food on that day.

1

We worked as a team against Sammy the Snake
until Sammy went back to his side of the lake.
He swam towards his home but I know he'll be back,
that Sammy is sly when he's on the attack.

I thought for a moment of what I might do
with the sun fading fast and my choices so few.

3

So I crawled up the bank and out of the lake
to see the lay of the land and to avoid a mistake.

Either I hide in the water for the rest of the night or hop through the dark until I see light.

But if I stay here I'll be trapped in the lake and won't stand a chance against Sammy the Snake.

So its best that I leave and head for that shed and
hope I find safety and a place to make bed.

But as I hopped toward the shed I saw someone I knew,
it was Bobo's wife Mimi home cooking some stew.

She said "Bobo has gone to see Freddie the Fish
when he saved Bobo's life I made Freddie a dish.
I sent him a bowl of my favorite stew
but I'm worried for Bobo when
Sammy's there too."

I told her about Sammy and my lucky escape
and she mentioned that Freddie had a similar scrape.
That's why I'm here. I left from the lake.
I almost was eaten by Sammy the Snake.

That's when I asked "could I please spend the night.
I'll be quiet as a mouse and leave at first light."
Mimi said "Yes, of course you can stay.
It's nice to have company when Bobo's away.

I too have been scared and I sure can't deny
that I've seen signs that Sammy's been lurking close by.
But we'll be safe in my home with little to fear.
Sammy's back at the lake and it's a long ways from here.

I have stew on the stove that I'd like you to try
and then for desert I have sweet black bird pie."
So I went in the house and sat down to eat
and thanked my friend Mimi for being so sweet.

But as I gave thanks I heard something strange.
Something was wrong outside on the range.

'Twas Ricky the Rabbit who burst through the door and hid by the hay across the barn floor.

"Hey Ricky, its Phillip, and Mimi the Mouse,
hop over here and come into the house."

14

"Why are you here and looking so pale?"
"Because Sammy the Snake is hot on my trail."

We all stood in silence as we eyed the barn door
and then we watched Sammy snake his way on the floor.

16

"Quick follow me" whispered Mimi the Mouse.
"I'll show you the way to the back of the house."

So Ricky the Rabbit joined Mimi and I
and we fled before eating the stew and the pie.
But as we ran out the back we slipped in some bog
so we asked for protection from Henry the Hog.

Then Bobo returned from down at the lake
while we were still hiding from Sammy the Snake.
He walked in his house but then he ran out the door
and hid in the hay across the barn floor.

19

So we stayed in the mud in Henry's Pigsty
and let Henry protect us with Sammy close by.
Then Sammy stopped chasing and I think I know why.
Sammy the Snake was eating my pie.

So I sneaked in the house to have a look-see
but the pie was all gone with only crumbs left for me.

I learned a good lesson that I'll never forget,
just leave Sammy pie and he won't be a threat.
It may not be rabbit or frog on the grill
but a big piece of pie seemed to give him a thrill.

There is an old saying that might really be true
and I think it's a lesson Sammy already knew.
When something comes easy there's no reason to push
because a bird in the hand is worth two in the bush.

23

Book #1 Jimmy the Giraffe

Book #2 Ricky and Bobo

Book #3 Terry and Freddie

Book #4 Sammy the Snake

Book #5 Phillip and Mimi

Book #6 Henry the Hog

Book #7 Lucy the Lion

Book #8 Big Ben the Bear

Book #9 Billy and Rocky

Book #10 Freddie and Eddie

Book #11 Grant the Grizzly

Book #12 Daisey the Deer

Book #13 Darla the Doe

Book #14 Tommy the Tiger

Book #15 Sugar Shane & the Twins

Book #16 Scottie and Mitch

Book #17 A Rescue Ranch Christmas

Book #18 Bobo and Clyde

Book #19 Brandon and Howie

Book #20 Bradley the Bronco

Book #21 Linus and Leslie

Book #22 Linus and Milo

Book #23 Milo and Mitch

Book #24 A Rescue Ranch Picnic

Book #25 Tommy and David

Book #26 David the Dingo

Book #27 Tommy and Isaac

Book #28 Isaac and Ben

Book #29 Isaac the Ibis

Book #30 Danny the Duck

Book #31 Bradley and the Birds

Book #32 Leo and the Critters

Book #33 Rocky's Return

Book #34 Eddie and Frankie

Book #35 Frankie the Fox

Book #36 Frankie and the Twins

Book #37 The Twins

Book #38 Bradley and Amber

Book #39 Henry and Ben

Book #40 Donald the Dragon

Book #41 Mother Mary Mouse

Book #42 Keith and RC

Book #43 Rocky and Sandy

Book #44 Sandy and the Jackals

Book #45 Donald and George

WEBSITES

rhyminganimaladventures.com

*** **PUBLISHED BOOKS ARE IN BOLD PRINT***